The school fair

Written by Lynne Burgess

Illustrated by Anne Parsons

Amy and Daniel were at the
school fair.
Daniel came with his dog Spike.
Daniel's mum and dad were helping
at the fair.

'I want to play all the games,'
said Daniel.

'So do I,' said Amy. 'But Spike
can't come.'

Daniel put Spike's lead over the fence.
'Good dog, Spike,' he said.

Amy and Daniel walked over to
one of the games.
'What do we have to do?'
asked Daniel.
'You must catch one of the ducks,'
said Daniel's dad.

So Daniel tried to catch a duck.
He tried and tried but he could not
catch a duck.

Then Amy had a go.

'Look at my duck,' she laughed.

'What do I get for catching a duck?'

'Here you are,' said Daniel's dad,
and he gave Amy a little red car.
'Look Daniel,' said Amy.
'I have got a little red car.'
Daniel was sad.
'I wish I had a car like that,' he said.

'Let's play this game now,' said Amy.

'What do we have to do?'
asked Daniel.

'You must get a hoop over a skittle,'
said Daniel's mum.

So Daniel tried to get a hoop
over a skittle.

He tried and tried but he could not
get a hoop to go over a skittle.

Then Amy had a go.

She tried and tried.

Then one of her hoops flew up and up

and came down over a skittle.

'Here you are,' said Daniel's mum,
and she gave Amy a little blue car.
'Look Daniel,' said Amy. 'Now I
have a blue car and a red car.'
Daniel was very sad.
'I wish I had a car,' he said.

'Let's go and play that game there,'
said Amy.

'You can,' said Daniel. 'I don't
want to. I want to go home.
I'm going to get Spike.'

Daniel walked over to the fence.
He could see Spike. But now there were
one... two... three... four... five... six
dogs.

When Spike saw Daniel coming,
he jumped up and down.
'Oh Spike!' said Daniel.
'What have you got there?'
Spike had a big rosette on his collar.

'Spike has got the prize for the
biggest dog at the fair,'
said Mrs Green.
She gave Daniel a big box.
'Here is your prize,' said Mrs Green.

Daniel opened the box as fast
as he could.
'Look Amy,' he laughed.
'I have got a big red car.
Good old Spike.'